MW01113743

The Adventures of the Little Prince

"By searching for what we think we need, we discover our strengths and capabilities and come to realize what we really need has been there all along."

-Rosemary Evans

Dedicated to my 11 grandsons
Drew
Jackson
Bryce
Jacob
Sheldon
Evan
Paxton
Tanner
Austin
Christian
and
Parker

Each one a True Prince!

The Adventures of The Little Prince

Recipient of:
Mom's Choice Awards Gold Medal for Excellence in Children's Literature and the Royal Dragonfly Book Awards First Place.

Copyright © 2013 by Rosemary R. Evans. All rights reserved.

No portion of this book may be reproduced, stored in a retrieval system, or transmitted in any form or by any means, without prior written permission.

Published by Wink Publishing - www.winkpublishing.com
Printed in China

Publisher's Cataloging-in-Publication Data

Evans, Rosemary R.
   The adventures of the little prince / written by Rosemary R. Evans ; illustrated by Erin Taylor.
      p. cm.
   ISBN: 978-1-61658-706-2 (hardcover)
   ISBN: 978-0-9885976-2-4 (e-book)
   1. Princes—Fiction. 2. Voyages and travels—Fiction. 3. Conduct of life—Fiction. 4. Picture books for children.
I. Taylor, Erin, ill. II. Title.
PZ7 .E89228 Ad 2013
[Fic]—dc23

2011920602

nce upon a time, a Little Prince lived in a castle with the King and Queen in a far away kingdom. All the people in the kingdom loved the King and Queen, because they were both so kind and brave and fair. The King was so happy to have The Little Prince as a son, and he often told The Little Prince that someday he would grow up to be the King. The Little Prince did not think that he wanted to be a King, and what he wanted more than anything else was to go on an adventure.

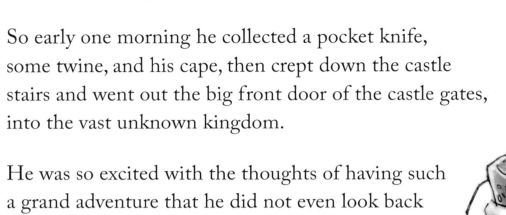

So early one morning he collected a pocket knife, some twine, and his cape, then crept down the castle stairs and went out the big front door of the castle gates, into the vast unknown kingdom.

He was so excited with the thoughts of having such a grand adventure that he did not even look back at the castle.

He walked and walked, and soon came around a bend in the road, where he saw a band of Gypsies. He had heard a little about Gypsies but he really hadn't seen any before. The leader of the Gypsies, seeing The Little Prince, decided to hold him for ransom.

The Little Prince said, "You can not hold me for ransom! I have left the castle for an adventure, and I want to join your band of Gypsies."

The leader of the Gypsies was so amazed at the boldness and the braveness of The Little Prince that he began to laugh. "You are a very brave young man! Indeed you may join us."

"What do Gypsies really do?" inquired The Little Prince. The leader laughed again and said to watch and learn. Many wagons and carriages passed along the road. The Gypsies would jump out from behind the trees, stop the wagons and carriages, and rob the people. It upset The Little Prince to see the Gypsies taking things that didn't belong to them, from these poor people.

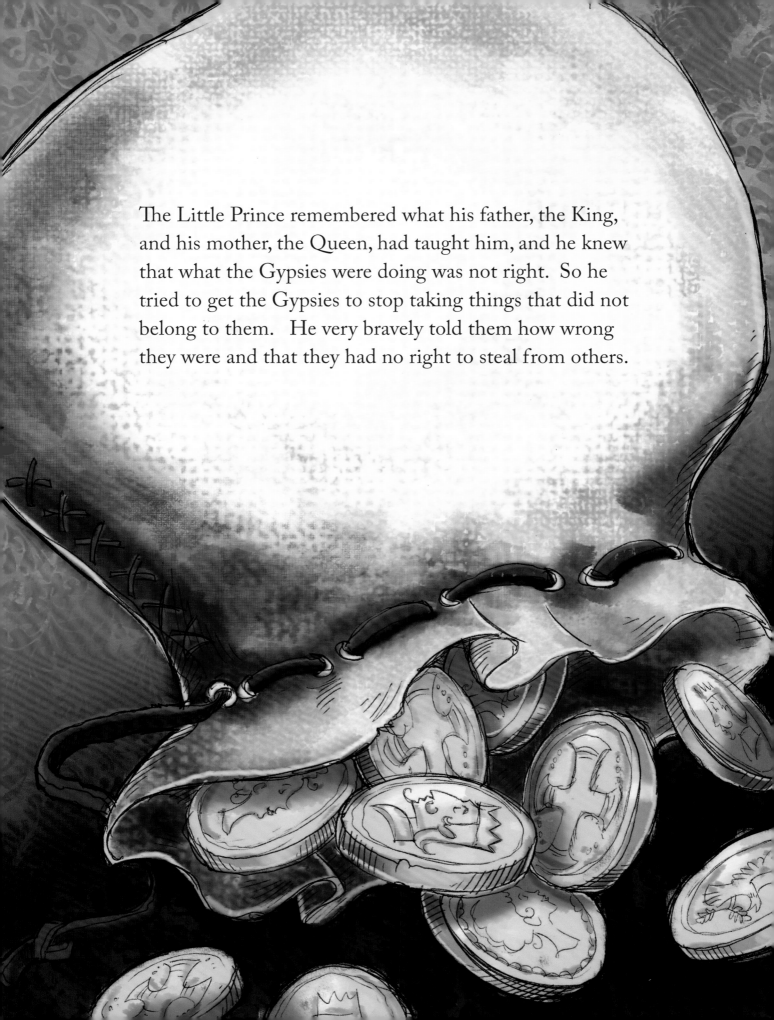

The Little Prince remembered what his father, the King, and his mother, the Queen, had taught him, and he knew that what the Gypsies were doing was not right. So he tried to get the Gypsies to stop taking things that did not belong to them. He very bravely told them how wrong they were and that they had no right to steal from others.

Hearing this over and over again, The Gypsies lost all
interest in The Little Prince, and forgot they wanted
him for a ransom. They were so annoyed by his
goodness that they asked him to leave.

Well, The Little Prince wasn't too happy with them
either, so off he went to find another adventure.

He walked and walked and came upon a little house in the woods. The Little Prince did not know that a lonely, old woman and her black cat lived in this little house. The townspeople thought because she lived by herself in the forest and had a black cat, that she must be a witch. So The Little Prince was quite startled when an old woman with a pointy chin and a pointy nose opened the door.

With a raspy voice she asked, "What are you doing coming to my door?" Very meekly The Little Prince asked if she could please give him a drink of water because he was so thirsty from walking for so long. The Little Prince noticed that the old woman had very kind eyes.

"Aren't you afraid of me," she asked, "Haven't you heard I'm a witch?"

The Little Prince replied, "Which witch?" and they both began to laugh.
They laughed and laughed until tears rolled down their cheeks.

"Well, aren't you a pleasant little fellow," the old woman said, and offered him not only water to drink but some of her delicious corn cake she had just taken out of the oven.

They had a nice visit and he promised that he would come back to see her again. She was happy for his company and The Little Prince was happy that he made a new friend.

She wrapped another piece of corn cake in a little cloth and gave it to him to take on his adventure. Thanking her, he put the corn cake in his satchel, and off he went.

After walking a little ways, he came to a river which wasn't very wide, and wasn't really a river, although it did look very big to The Little Prince. He wondered how he could ever get across. He looked around and saw some small branches, and he had an idea! He decided to cut the leaves off the branches. Then he tied the branches together with the twine he brought with him from the castle, and made a small raft. He used one of the branches as an oar, and off he went across the river to the other side.

When he got to the other side he saw a beautiful young woman cutting some wood.

"What are you doing young maiden?" asked The Little Prince. The maiden said, "I am cutting some wood for my stove so I can cook food for my hungry little children. My husband is away and I ran out of wood."

So The Little Prince helped her collect the wood and then carried it to her small cottage which was a little ways off.

"You are so kind, and such a great worker. I have not seen such ambition in such a young lad," said the fair young maiden, and she leaned over and kissed The Little Prince on the forehead. The Little Prince said that he was happy he could help her and then he picked up his satchel and waved goodbye.

He soon came to a large ravine. "How will I ever cross over this large ravine?" he wondered. He sat on the ground to think things over, when he noticed that the sun was setting and it was getting dark.

The Little Prince was beginning to miss his mother and father, and decided he didn't want to sleep on the cold, hard ground. He thought that his nice, warm feather bed in the palace would be a good place to sleep. He decided maybe he wouldn't worry about being a King just yet and just go back to the castle and be a Prince.

So he started walking back to the castle. After he had walked for what seemed like a long time, he came upon a man sitting on the ground. "What, sir, are you doing?" asked The Little Prince. The man explained that he was riding his horse when suddenly they ran into a tree branch and he fell off his horse, and his horse had run away.

"Oh," said The Little Prince, "perhaps I could help you find your horse. I have a little corn cake that I think your horse would like, so if we put it on the ground and walk away, I think your horse will come back."

So the man and The Little Prince sat very quietly and talked in very soft voices, and after a while they heard the chomping of the horse eating the corn cake. The man was able to get his horse and was able to continue on his journey.

"What a helpful and giving young lad you are," said the man and he thanked The Little Prince. The Little Prince continued to walk and as he came around the bend, he could see the castle not so far away.

He reached the big gates that lead to the courtyard of the castle. He rang the big bell at the castle wall and the huge gates swung open wide.

When The Little Prince walked inside, what a surprise he had!
In the castle courtyard, he saw the Gypsies, the old woman,
the young maiden, and the man with his horse. They
all began to clap and cheer for The Little Prince
to welcome him home. The doors to the
castle opened wide and the King
and Queen ran to greet the
Little Prince.

"Welcome home!" said the King. "All of the people you met and helped on your journey have told us of your kindness, bravery, and unselfishness. You will make a wonderful King one day, and all that I have will be yours. But for now, we are just so happy to have you home!"

And that is exactly what did happen. The Little Prince grew into a fine, handsome, kind man, and became a great King who was loved by all the people.

Rosemary Evans lives in Lake Oswego, Oregon with her husband Richard. She is the mother of 4 children, and grandmother of 14.

She has written 4 children's books:

"The Little Princesses Magical Party", inspired by her three granddaughters. "Abrielle and Annelise stayed overnight, and we were having so much fun that they almost missed their bedtime story." Rosemary promised the girls that she would tell them a story, if they stayed in bed, left the lights off, and were very quiet. So she made up a story about two little princesses who had a magical party and learned what it really means to be a true princess.

"The Adventures of the Little Prince", inspired by her 11 grandsons. This story is about a young prince who wants to have a grand adventure, more than learning how to be a king. Very early one morning, he leaves the castle and sets off on his first adventure. On the way, he meets gypsies, a 'witch' who is really a lonely old lady, a young maiden who needs help, and a man whose horse has run away. The young prince finds many opportunities to help others and discovers that he has the qualities to become a great king after all.

"Teeny Tiny Tina the Teeny Tiny Tooth Fairy" One of Rosemary's granddaughters told her that when a tooth comes out and you leave it for the tooth fairy, she leaves you money. It inspired the author to write her first story about Teeny Tiny Tina, a cute little fairy who really, really wanted to be a tooth fairy, but everyone told her she was too teeny. You will enjoy discovering how Tina finally becomes a tooth fairy, in this wonderful, fun book.

"Teeny Tiny Tina and Her Teeny Tiny Pet" In this second Tina book you can read about Tina and her favorite pet named Kat. Tina's sisters Annabelle and Rosebud tell her that her pet is going to change into a butterfly. She goes to great lengths to try to stop the process. What happens to Kat? How does Tina discover that change is not something to fear? Read all about her adventures with Kat in this fun new book.

Her children's books can be ordered from Wink Publishing, by sending an email to **info@winkpublishing.com** or on Tina's website, **www.TinaToothFairy.com**. They will soon be available at major bookstores across the country.

Erin Taylor is a freelance illustrator who loves to draw, visit the zoo and travel. When she isn't on an airplane she can be found painting away with her husband Adam. To see more of her work, or to contact her about illustrating your next book, visit **www.ErinTaylorIllustrator.com**. Rosemary says "I am thrilled that my illustrator captured all four of my stories exactly as I envisioned them."

Rosemary is also the author of:

"Live Your Perfect Weight – The Missing Link to Weight Loss"
"Healthy Body – Healthy Skin"
"Change Your Script and Change Your Life"

You can order these three books at
www.LiveYourPerfectWeight.com.